Postman

and the goat's supper

John Cunliffe
Illustrated by Stuart Trotter
from the original television designs by Ivor Wood

*Hodder
Children's
Books*

a division of Hodder Headline plc

One morning, Pat had a parcel for Miss Hubbard.
It was a big, soft, squashy parcel.
"I wonder what it is?" said Pat to Jess. "It feels like
a cushion."

Miss Hubbard was pleased to see her parcel.
"Have a cup of coffee," she said, "while I open it."

It wasn't a cushion at all.
It was a blue jumper.
She tried it on.
"Lovely," she said,
"just the thing for wearing
on my bike on chilly days.
It's from Cousin Nellie,
in Nelson."

"What a kind cousin," said Pat. "Does she knit
things for men?"
"I don't think so," said Miss Hubbard.
"Pity," said Pat. "Well, thanks for the coffee.
I'll be on my way now. Bye!"

Pat saw the blue jumper again, one evening, when he was going home after choir-practice. It was hanging on Miss Hubbard's washing-line.
"She's gone to bed and forgotten it," said Pat. "But it'll be all right. There's no wind to blow it away."

There was no wind, but there was a hungry goat. No-one saw it jump over the wall, looking for something to eat for its supper. Its bright eyes spotted the jumper, and it trotted over to see what it was.

Then it did what some goats will do. It tugged and it nibbled...

and chewed at it...

and ate a great chunk
out of the sleeve. Oh,
what a mischief that goat was!

It went all about Miss Hubbard's garden, nibbling at this and that – flowers of all sorts, lettuce, a cabbage-leaf – and poking its nose everywhere.

It knocked a bucket over, and gave Miss Hubbard a dreadful fright.

Worst of all was when she got up next morning and saw the hole in the hedge, and then saw the hole in her new jumper!

"Oh, my jumper," wailed Miss Hubbard.

"It was my favourite."

When Pat came, he said,
"Don't you worry. Just write to Cousin Nellie. She'll be able to knit a new sleeve, in no time at all."

Before the end of the week, there was a post-card
from Nellie.
"It's not good news," said Pat, as he gave the card
to Miss Hubbard. "She says that she has no more
wool of that colour."
"Oh, deary me, it's just what I feared."
"Don't take on," said Pat. "I'll keep a look out.
There must be some of it somewhere."

R. Hubbard
ands Farm Cottage
ale
Britain

Pat tied a strand of the wool on his steering-wheel, to remind him. One day, he called on Granny Dryden, and there she was, knitting a scarf for Ted Glen: a blue scarf.

"The very same colour!" said Pat, running to get
the wool from his van. It was a perfect match.
"Can you knit sleeves?" said Pat.
"I was knitting sleeves before you were born," said
Granny Dryden.

Pat told her all about Miss Hubbard and her jumper. "Sounds like one of Alf's goats," said Granny Dryden. "I have a lot of that colour. I was wondering what to do with it."

Granny Dryden knitted a new sleeve, and Miss
Hubbard said her mended jumper was like new.
Never again did she leave it out to dry
at night.

As for Alf's goat… Alf mended the hole in the fence, and it had to make do with oats and grass for its supper after that!

More Postman Pat adventures: